A PARRAGON BOOK

Published by Parragon Book Service Ltd,
Units 13-17, Avonbridge Trading Estate, Atlantic Road,
Avonmouth, Bristol BS11 9QD

Produced by The Templar Company plc,
Pippbrook Mill, London Road, Dorking, Surrey RH4 1JE

Edited by Caroline Repchuk
Designed by Mark Summersby

Printed and bound in Great Britain

ISBN 0 - 75250 - 757 - 5

NURSERY RHYME LAND

Written by Caroline Repchuk
Illustrated by Maggie Downer

||| •PARRAGON• |||

Welcome to Nursery Rhyme Land!

You have entered a world filled with fun and laughter - the wonderful world of Nursery Rhymes! As you turn the pages some of your favourite nursery rhymes will spring to life on this journey through Nursery Rhyme Land. Look at each picture and you will spot all sorts of familiar characters. You'll find a list of things to discover on each spread, some of which will be harder to find than others. Try making your own list too, of all the extra characters from the rhymes that you find. And don't forget that dear old Mother Goose is hidden in every scene - she likes to keep a watchful eye over everyone. See if you can find her on all the pages. Happy searching!

Girls and boys come out to play

Wee Willy Winkie is running around the town checking to see if the girls and boys are in their beds.

Can you find him, and can you also find:

- **Children playing a ring o'roses**
- **Georgie Porgie**

- **A see-saw**
- **An owl**
- **Two teddies**

Down on the farm

Old Macdonald is busy looking after his farm. See if you can find him and some other favourite nursery rhyme characters.

Can you spot:

- **Mary and her little lamb**
- **Hickety Pickety, a black hen**
- **A dapple grey pony**
- **Three little pigs**
- **Three blind mice**
- **A pussy in the well**

In the meadow

Can you find Little Miss Muffet and can you spot what is about to frighten her away?

Can you also find:

- **Baa Baa Black Sheep**
- **Little Bo Peep**
- **Six rabbits**

- **The little boy who lives down the lane**

In the palace

Old King Cole is a merry old soul — see how his palace is full of fun! Can you find his pipe and bowl?

Can you also find:

- **Three fiddlers**
- **The Knave of Hearts**
- **A clothes peg**
- **A mouse**
- **Twenty-four blackbirds**
- **A cat**

To market, to market...

The market at Banbury Cross is full of hustle and bustle.
See if you can find a fine lady on a white horse there.

Can you also spot:

- **Banbury Cross**
- **Little Jack Horner**
- **Simple Simon**

- **The little pig who went to market**

FOR SALE

PIES FOR SALE

All around the town

The Lion and the Unicorn are fighting to rule the town.
Can you see what the townspeople are giving them?

And can you find:

- **Yankee Doodle**
- **The baker's shop**
- **A crown**

- **Goosey Goosey Gander**
- **Three barking dogs**
- **Three beggars in rags**

In the garden

Mary's garden is full of lovely and unusual things. Can you see her row of pretty maids?

And can you also find:

- Peter Piper
- A mulberry bush
- A partridge
- An itsy bitsy spider
- Someone going round and round the garden

In the kitchen

Old Mother Hubbard hasn't filled up her cupboard, and so she can't give her poor dog a bone. Her kitchen is full of some favourite nursery rhyme characters though.

Can you find:

- Jack Sprat
- A cake marked with 'B'
- A kettle
- Little Tommy Tucker
- A hungry dog
- Two mice

Along the road

A walk through Nursery Rhyme Land can be quite an adventure. Count all the characters that are on the road today.

And see if you can find:

- **The piper's son**
- **Three young rats**
- **Seven wives**
- **Three young ducks**

St. IVES
10
MILES

On the sea

Rub-a-dub, dub, three men in a tub, are sailing on the sea. Do you know who they are?

And can you find:

- **Three ships**
- **Betty Blue's missing shoe**
- **Bobby Shaftoe**
- **The owl and the pussycat**

Twinkle, twinkle

As night-time falls over Nursery Rhyme Land
look carefully and you'll see the cow jumping
over the moon.

Can you also see:

- **A laughing dog**
- **A cradle**
- **A twinkling star**
- **A Wise Old Owl**

Up hill and down dale

Jack and Jill go up the hill, but find they have company!

Can you find:

- **A Grand Old Duke**
- **An old woman**
- **A ladybird**
- **A well**
- **A bottle of vinegar**
- **Three rabbits**

VINEGAR

Home sweet home

There was an old woman who lived in a shoe...
see if you can find her amongst all her children.

And see if you can also find:

- **Little Tommy Tittlemouse**
- **The house that Jack built**
- **A crooked cat**
- **Peter the pumpkin eater's wife**

Come blow your horn

The cornfield should be quiet and peaceful, but Humpty Dumpty has fallen off the wall, the kittens have lost their mittens whilst out for a walk, and a cow has got lost in the corn!

See if you can find:

- **Six mittens**
- **Little Boy Blue**
- **A cow**
- **Humpty Dumpty**

Child's play

It's nightime now and nearly all of the children in Nursery Rhyme Land are fast asleep. But two little girls are still awake playing.

Can you spot:

- Little pussy
- A mouse
- A spinning top
- Lazy John
- A book of rhymes
- A horrid girl